HILLSIDE LIVE!. . .

''So, Dylan, from now on the most important thing to us is getting the band in that movie. Deal?''

''Deal.'' As I shook Chris's hand, I felt a little twinge of conscience. I told myself I was just doing this for the sake of the band—but was I? Or was the band just an excuse? Did I secretly want to see myself as a star?

Maybe I'm just as geeky as the rest of them, I thought. Just as big a fool as Matt, as phony as Courtney, as starstruck as Brooke . . .

Nah.

Chris went on his way. I stopped by the bathroom to check my hair in the mirror.

Read all the **FIFTEEN**™ books:

FIFTEEN

Hillside Live!

FIFTEEN™

Hillside Live!

By Emily James

PUBLISHERS · GROSSET & DUNLAP · NEW YORK
in association with Nickelodeon Books™

CHAPTER 1

Arseman

"**C**OURTNEY, WHAT ARE you doing? Your ice cream is melting." I slid into the booth opposite Courtney, who was busy writing in a notebook—so busy, in fact, it seemed she'd forgotten all about the dish of strawberry ice cream sitting in front of her.

She looked up at me and slowly focused on my face, as if just waking up from a dream. "Hi, Arseman," Courtney said, shoving the dish toward me. "You can have it. I don't want it."

It was early one Friday afternoon, and the Avalon was packed with the usual lunchtime crowd. Blocking out the background noise, I picked up a spoon and dipped it into the ice cream.

"What are you working on?" I asked after licking the spoon. "You're missing a great dish of ice cream, by the way."

Without looking up, she said, "Just one minute, Arseman. I'm almost done." She scribbled a few more sentences.

Everybody knows Courtney's a really good writer. She spends a lot of time working on poetry and stuff like that.

I shrugged and slurped another spoonful of ice cream, just watching Courtney concentrate. She has pretty, shoulder-length brown curls that she usually wears tied back with a scarf. That day's scarf was a funky pink and green paisley print. Finally I tugged on the end of it, and she lifted her head.

"Hey," I said. "You'll get your work done. You always do."

Courtney sighed and put her pen down. "It's not homework," she said. "It's my diary."

"Whoops," I said. "Sorry I interrupted. Want some privacy?"

"No, that's okay." She shut her notebook. "I'm finished with today's entry. Actually, there's not much to write about. My life is so boring."

"Courtney, how can you say that? Your life isn't boring."

"Oh, no? Tell me what's interesting about it."

I thought hard, but I honestly was drawing a blank. "Umm . . ." I said, stalling for time.

"See?" Courtney said. "You can't come up with a single interesting thing to say about my life."

"Courtney, everybody's life has slow periods. This isn't the movies, after all. It can't be exciting every second of the day. Look, my life isn't very interesting right now, either."

"What about the band? That's kind of interesting."

I'm in a band with two guys in our class, Chris and Dylan. I'm the singer. I guess it sounds glamorous, but actually I spend a lot of time in Dylan's garage, just listening to Chris and Dylan argue over which songs to play. I love to sing, but I hate watching those two fight.

Courtney said, "I wish my life were more dramatic, more romantic—the way it is in books."

I took another spoonful of ice cream and said, "I know what you mean. Don't worry, Courtney.

Something's bound to come along and shake things up. Any minute now, I'll bet."

She laughed. "I hope you're right."

"Hey, Arseman—Courtney." I looked up to see Dylan standing by our booth, though I would have known that cool tone of voice anywhere. "Got any room for me? This place is packed today."

I slid over to let Dylan sit down. He's a tall, thin guy with longish brown hair that's always falling in his eyes. He was wearing his usual outfit: ripped blue jeans, a white t-shirt, and a black leather jacket. When I first met Dylan, I thought he was sullen and kind of moody, but I understand him better now. He's really pretty sensitive, but he doesn't want anybody to know it, so he tries to cover it up by acting cool. Of course, if I said this to him he'd totally deny it.

"Want to come over after school and jam today, Arseman?" Dylan asked me. He glanced at Courtney and added, "You can come, too, if you feel like it. You know, just to hang out."

Courtney looked uncomfortable. Her younger brother, Billy, used to be the drummer for the band, but Dylan and Chris kicked him out. It was Chris's idea. Dylan always liked Billy, but he had to admit that Billy just wasn't that good. I tried to stay out of the whole thing, myself.

"I don't know, Dylan," Courtney said. "It might hurt Billy's feelings if he knew I was hanging out with the band."

Dylan nodded. "Sure. I understand. Anyway, Arseman, how about you? You up for it?"

"Sure. I've got a few new songs I'd like to try out."

"Great." Then Dylan's expression changed suddenly, from relaxed and pleasant to irritated and annoyed. He slumped in his seat and said, "Look who's headed this way—Miss Troublemaker herself."

I looked up and saw Brooke gliding casually toward us. At least, she was trying to *look* casual; but Brooke always has a purpose—usually a hidden one—behind anything she does. Her short, light brown hair was stylishly combed, and she was wearing a blue leather miniskirt, a silk t-shirt, stockings, matching blue pumps, and lots of carefully applied makeup. Brooke doesn't know the meaning of the word casual. She walked up to our table and stopped suddenly, as if she had just noticed us.

"Oh, hello, Dylan," she said. She just nodded

at me and Courtney. Then she sat down next to Courtney, nudging her into the corner of the booth so that she could have more room. "You don't mind if I sit here, do you? There isn't another seat to be found in the whole place."

She flashed a blinding smile at Dylan, who was still slumped unhappily in his seat. Dylan makes it totally obvious when he doesn't like somebody. He sat up and slid out of the booth.

"I've got a class in a few minutes. Gotta go. See you after school, Arseman."

"See you, Dylan." He left the Avalon.

Now Brooke turned her blazing smile on me. " 'See you after school, Arseman'? Is something going on here I should know about?"

"Like what, Brooke?" I asked.

She leaned forward in her seat and said, "I'm not stupid, Arseman. I can figure things out for myself. It's Friday, and you're meeting Dylan after school. That sounds like a date to me."

Courtney was trying not to laugh. Brooke could be such a fool sometimes.

"It's not a date, Brooke," I said, trying not to sound impatient with her. "It's just a band rehearsal. No big deal."

"You sure see a lot of Dylan because of that band," Brooke said.

"Yeah, and I see a lot of Chris, too," I said. "Stop trying to stir things up, Brooke. You know there's nothing between me and Dylan."

She smirked. "I was just checking. I like to keep tabs on these things."

"Why do you care whether Arseman and Dylan are dating or not?" Courtney asked. "Maybe *you* have a thing for Dylan, yourself?"

Brooke stiffened. "I do not," she huffed. "Whatever gave you such a ridiculous idea?"

Courtney shrugged in mock innocence. "Just checking," she said sweetly. "I like to keep tabs on these things."

Brooke was fuming. "I know why you're so interested, Courtney. Everybody knows you've had a crush on Dylan for ages. I guess you never got over him, even after he turned you down *flat.*"

Courtney frowned, but I was determined not to let Brooke have the last word. A while back Courtney *had* liked Dylan, but she was over him now.

"Courtney has moved on to new things," I said. "Maybe you should, too, Brooke."

I could almost see the smoke coming out of her ears. "If you think that I care one bit about that ratty guitar player, then you've got another thing coming!"

She stood up and stormed off. Courtney and I couldn't help laughing.

"What a lame comeback," Courtney said. "I think she *does* have a thing for him."

"Me, too," I agreed. "She's so transparent."

When Courtney and I returned to school that afternoon, we heard that Mr. Phipps, the principal, had called a special assembly. That was a surprise. Special assemblies don't happen very often, so I was really curious.

The auditorium was completely full when Mr. Phipps walked up to the stage. Mr. Phipps is short, chubby, and bald. "We'll be having a visitor for the next week and a half," he announced. "His name is Jack Rhea. He's a graduate of Hillside, and now he's a film director. Mr. Rhea is making a documentary about high-school students, and he's going to shoot it right here at Hillside—starting Monday."

A roar went through the auditorium. A movie! Right here at Hillside!

"Mr. Rhea wants you all to act naturally, to be yourselves. There will be cameras all over the school, and the camera operators will be as inconspicuous as possible. There may even be microphones hidden around campus. There will be a lot of times when you may not realize you're being filmed. So I hope you'll all be on your best behavior—uh, your best *natural* behavior."

Some of the kids snickered. Their best "natural" behavior definitely wasn't good enough for Mr. Phipps.

Mr. Phipps wiped the sweat from his forehead with a handkerchief. "I think you all know what I mean. Please don't do anything to embarrass your friends or your school. We want to show the world what a great school we have here at Hillside. Right?"

Silence.

Mr. Phipps smiled his nervous smile—the one he gives us when he feels as though he's losing control. Finally he answered his own question. "Right. Mr. Rhea and his crew will be here all next week until the following Tuesday, so many school events that are scheduled for that week—the Academic Olympics, the gymnastics meet, the volleyball tournament, the art show, and so on—will be filmed as they happen. I hope that won't make any of you nervous. Just try to forget that the cameras are there, and do your best. . . .

"Well, that's it for today. See you all Monday morning."

Everybody started talking at once. Courtney turned to me and said, "We're going to be in a documentary, Arseman. So much for life not being like the movies. Cool, huh?" Courtney spoke pretty calmly, considering this was just the thing she'd been wishing for. Then she adjusted her scarf, picked up her backpack, and stood up to leave.

I stood up, too. "It's cool," I said. "But it's a little scary. I'm not sure I like the idea of cameras recording everything I do."

"I'm sure they won't record *everything*," said Ashley in her soft voice. Ashley is a good friend of ours. She's petite, blond, and gets straight A's. "After all, we have a right to our privacy."

"Privacy. Yeah, right," Chris said. He and Dylan had swaggered up behind Ashley and jumped into our conversation. "This guy's a big deal. He can do whatever he wants."

"I don't care what he does," said Dylan. "I couldn't care less about some jerk doing a documentary."

"I don't have a problem with acting natural," Courtney said. "I just hope other kids won't flip out over this and start showing off and stuff."

As if on cue, Brooke ran up to us just then, clutching her books to her chest and gushing, "Isn't it *thrilling!* I'm finally going to be discovered!"

These next couple of weeks were going to be weird.

CHAPTER 2

Brooke

As soon as I heard Mr. Phipps's announcement that Friday, I knew my life was going to be changed forever. It was fate. I always knew I'd be famous, but I thought I'd have to wait until I finished high school, and then maybe move to New York or Hollywood and at least *audition* a few times. But here was Jack Rhea, film director, right here at Hillside. It was as if he'd been sent by my guardian angel, just to find me.

That afternoon I ran right home. The way I saw it, I had a lot of work to do over the weekend. I mean, I hadn't expected my big break to come so soon, and I wasn't ready, not at all!

I dropped my books on the floor—where they belong, as far as I'm concerned—and went straight to my vanity table for a good long look in the mirror. I know I always look attractive. But a girl has to take stock of herself once in a while, assess her good points and her faults—though I don't have many faults, if I do say so myself—and make changes as she needs them. Any fashion magazine will tell you that. Well, I saw right away that I needed a new haircut. I've got thick, short hair that is just stunning, but it needs regular trims to keep it in perfect shape. Also, I was ready for a whole new makeup kit. I was getting pretty tired of that pinkish shade of lipstick I'd been wearing, and if I changed lipsticks I'd have to change everything else, too. And then there were my clothes. . . . I do have great taste, of course, but I definitely needed some new clothes, pronto.

My totally annoying little sister, Amanda, chose just that moment to barge into my room.

"What are you doing?" she said with her Little-Miss-Know-It-All sneer, which drives me crazy. "Kissing the mirror again?"

I ignored her nasty comment, as usual. "If you must know, Amanda," I said coolly, "I'm getting ready to spend the whole weekend making myself even more glamorous than I already am. I've got to look my best on Monday morning when the cameras start rolling."

She started laughing, the little brat, and didn't stop for several minutes. When she finally caught her breath, she pointed to all the makeup on my vanity table and said, "This is your idea of acting natural?"

"It's natural for *me*," I said. "It's *natural* for the star of a movie to be a little more glamorous than everybody else."

Then she started laughing again. I hate that. People think I'm mean to her, but if they had to live with her they'd be mean, too.

"Brooke, they're making a documentary about high school. What makes you think *you'll* be the star of it? You don't do any activities, you're not on any athletic teams, you don't get good grades . . ."

I interrupted her. "You're forgetting one crucial point, Amanda. Lots of kids do sports and activities. Big deal. But let's face it. I'm basically the center of all social life at Hillside."

"Oh, *please*," was the best answer the twerp could come up with. What else could she say? She couldn't deny the obvious, could she?

"I can't take any more of this," she said. "I only came in here because Mom wants me to tell you we're having company for dinner tonight. And I think you'll find our guest very interesting."

"Oh?" I said, picking up a mascara wand and giving my lashes an extra coat. "Who?"

"An old friend of Dad's from his Hillside days," said Amanda in a teasing voice. "I think his name is . . . Jack Rhea."

The mascara fell to the table with a clink. I had to make sure I had heard the girl right. I stood up and faced her, grabbing her by the shoulders. "Who? Who did you say is coming over for dinner tonight?"

"Ow! Let go of me." I let go of her bony shoulders, and she said his name again. "Jack Rhea."

"Jack Rhea! The director?"

"That's what I said. So you'd better be ready to eat at 7:30."

She left the room and slammed the door shut behind her. I didn't care. She had just brought me the best news I'd ever heard. Jack Rhea was an old friend of Dad's! Jack Rhea was coming here for dinner! It was my guardian angel in action! Now I knew for sure—it was meant to be. First, the announcement in school, and now this! There was no doubt in my mind: I was on my way to movie stardom. Look out, Michelle Pfeiffer!

By the time my father called me to dinner, I didn't look too bad. I was dressed as well as could be expected, considering I didn't have time to go shopping before dinner. I mean, I'd only had three hours' notice! I wore my slinky green silk dress. It shows off my eyes, and I think it makes me look older and more sophisticated. I stood at the top of the stairs and took a deep breath. Prepare yourself, Jack Rhea, I thought. You are about to meet the future superstar of all time.

Jack Rhea wasn't quite how I pictured a director to be. First of all, he didn't *look* much like a director. He came to dinner in jeans, a button-down shirt, and a sports jacket. I mean, my own father was dressed more elegantly! And I didn't expect him to have a beard—and a gray beard at that. He looked more like a college professor than a Hollywood director. But then I thought, well, Steven Spielberg has a beard, so I guess it's okay.

Amanda looked like a dweeb in her little schoolgirl jumper. Next to her, I must've been a knockout.

My father introduced us all to Jack, and then we sat down to dinner. Things were a little awkward at first, so I took it upon myself to get the ball rolling. "So," I said to Jack in my most mature manner, "I hear you're making a movie at Hillside High. What an interesting concept."

I could see Amanda out of the corner of my eye looking ready to barf, but I decided just to shut her out. I couldn't let her distract me from my mission.

"Yes," Jack said. "I'm making a documentary about high-school students today: what their lives are really like, what's important to them, what kinds of relationships they have with one another. . . ."

It sounded perfectly awful. The man needed me more than he knew.

"You know, *Jack*, I don't want to brag, but I think you could ask anyone and they'd tell you I'm the quintessential Hillside girl. I'm very popular—friends with just about everyone, in fact. And even though I'm the leader of the most exclusive clique in school—"

"Yeah," Amanda muttered under her stinky breath. "Your clique is so exclusive it only has one person in it."

I pretended that she hadn't spoken. "—I'm not the least bit snobby, and I make a point of reaching out to all the students in the school, even those who might not be as cool as I am."

"That's very admirable, Brooke," Jack said. He smiled at me, and I began to feel better.

"If you want a look at the most interesting people and places at Hillside," I continued, "all you have to do is follow me around with your camera, Jack. Every minute of my life is packed with drama. It'll make a great movie."

Amanda rolled her eyes.

Luckily, Jack wasn't paying any attention to her. "I'd be very interested in seeing what you do at school, Brooke," he said. "What about your boyfriend? What's he like?"

Boyfriend? Did I mention a boyfriend? I didn't think so. But if Jack Rhea wanted me to have a boyfriend, then I had a boyfriend.

"Maybe we could find a high-school couple with real screen presence," Jack went on. He seemed to be thinking aloud now. "I could focus on the two of them—you know, get the girl's point of view, then the boy's. The typical Hillside couple. . . ."

Yes—I liked the sound of that. But to be one half of Hillside's typical couple, I needed a boyfriend—fast. Well, I did already have someone in mind. He wasn't my boyfriend yet—in fact, he wasn't even my friend—but I knew he'd be perfect.

"My boyfriend isn't exactly the type of guy you'd expect me to go out with," I told Jack. Amanda was paying close attention now. She knew I didn't have a boyfriend.

"Oh? What sort of guy is he?"

"He's gorgeous—don't get me wrong. But he's a bit of a rebel—a rocker. I've always gone out with the clean-cut jock types before, but he just wouldn't leave me alone until I went out with him. He's crazy about me, and now I wouldn't want any other kind of guy."

"Hmmm," said Jack. "The rebel and the rich girl. That's always a good angle."

"I love it!" I said. "Wait until you meet him. The two of us together will light up the screen!"

Jack said, "Uh-huh. Say, could somebody pass me the rolls?"

Amanda couldn't keep her mouth shut any longer. "Who are you talking about?" she asked me.

I gave her my sweetest smile. "Why, you know, Amanda. My boyfriend. Dylan."

CHAPTER 3

<u>Dylan</u>

I REALLY DON'T mind school that much, as long as nobody bothers me. I like to do things my own way, to be left alone. So I wasn't sure how I felt on Friday afternoon when Mr. Phipps made that announcement about Jack Rhea and the movie. Cameras everywhere—that didn't sound so great to me. Just one more way for me to get caught cutting class or something.

But that wasn't the worst part. I had a bad feeling that things wouldn't be normal for a while, and I was right.

I saw the director on the street, scouting locations. He was an old guy, at least as old as my father. Nobody that old can make a good movie about high school, I thought. No way. He'll probably show everybody playing sports and going to dances and taking tests, but he won't show what high school is *really* like. He won't show all the snobby things kids do to each other, or people having arguments in the halls, or talking to each other at the Avalon, or fighting with their parents, or sitting alone playing the guitar. I was sure that the documentary was going to be nothing but a fake.

I was even more sure when I got to school on Monday morning. The camera crew kept turning up all over the place. They tried to stay out of our way, but you couldn't help but notice them—in the hallways, in the cafeteria, in the gym, in the classrooms. I hoped there wasn't one hiding in the bathroom. People were tripping over wires and stuff. And everybody in school, the kids I grew up with, all of a sudden they were like zombies. I hardly knew them. It was like they took one look at those cameras and forgot who they were.

Take Courtney. She's really nice. I'd never tell her this to her face, but I always kind of respected her because she is such a good writer and never phony. But the day those cameras came to Hillside, I saw a side of Courtney I'd never seen before.

I was standing by my locker, just watching the scene, when I saw Courtney go running up to Arseman, all worked up over something.

"Arseman, wait till you hear this!" she said.

"What?" said Arseman. I guess she likes a good piece of gossip as much as the next person.

Courtney started in. "Well, Matt was walking past Ms. Johnson's office, and guess who was sitting. . . ."

All of sudden, Courtney stopped talking. She was staring over Arseman's shoulder, at a tall woman in jeans running a movie camera. The camera was pointed right at Courtney.

A change came over Courtney when she saw that camera. It was like she was possessed. Her face sort of froze, and then it changed expression. She drew her mouth into a snooty little pucker and raised her eyebrows in this strange way that reminded me of Mr. Vogel, the librarian.

Arseman said, "Courtney, what is it? Who was sitting in Ms. Johnson's office?"

"Oh, Arseman," said Courtney in this weird new voice. It was almost like an English accent. "You know me better than *that*. I don't spread gossip. As George Eliot once wrote, 'Gossip is a sort of smoke that comes from the dirty tobacco-pipes of those who diffuse it: it proves nothing but the bad taste of the smoker.' "

I couldn't believe it. Where had Courtney come up with *that?* I mean, I knew Courtney read a lot, but what was this stuff about dirty tobacco pipes?

I could tell that Arseman was blown away, too. She said, "Courtney! What's come over you?"

Courtney said, "Nothing whatsoever, my good friend. Why do you ask?" And then she swirled around and kind of floated down the hallway with her long skirt trailing behind her.

Arseman saw me standing nearby and looked at me. She didn't say a word—I guess she was too shocked—but I could tell she was wondering what had just happened there. I pointed to the camera behind her. She turned around, looked at it, and then turned back to me. "So that's what it is," she said, shaking her head. "Unbelievable."

I thought so, too. I thought Courtney would be the last person to freak out over this movie thing. Her gossiping with Arseman might have been silly, but at least it was normal. This George Eliot stuff was definitely *not* normal.

And that was just the beginning. As I went to

my morning classes, I saw one weird and amazing thing after another. Of course, I should have expected weirdness from that bonehead jock, Matt. All of a sudden he was running around in his varsity jacket, carrying a basketball with him wherever he went. He dribbled it down the halls, bounced it against the walls, tried to make flashy shots into the trash cans, bonked a couple of kids in the head by mistake . . . All in all he acted like the jerk he normally is, times ten. And his little sister, Erin, was just as crazy. She was running through the halls with her friend Lea. Every time they saw a camera—which was about every five seconds—they'd start whispering to each other and run away.

The place was a zoo. I just watched, and swore I wouldn't be caught dead acting that way. I wasn't going to change anything about myself just because some guy was making a movie.

Then at lunchtime, as I was sitting in the cafeteria eating a sandwich and trying to ignore everyone else, Chris showed up. He sat down next to me. I had a feeling he had something he wanted to talk to me about. Chris is a short, dark-haired guy with a kind of arrogant way about him. Sometimes we get along, but a lot of times we don't.

I nodded toward Matt, who had just done

some kind of fancy basketball jump and landed right on his sister's foot. "Did you ever see such a bunch of morons?" I asked Chris.

"Huh?" Chris replied. "Never." He squirmed a little, but he didn't say anything else.

"Something on your mind?" I asked him.

"Yeah. This movie."

I put down my sandwich. I was too disgusted to eat any more. "Oh, no," I said. "Not you, too."

"Just listen, Dylan. You may not care about the movie. But you care about the band, don't you?"

"Yeah, I care about the band," I said. "So what?"

"So think about it. This documentary is going to be shown on television. Millions of people will see it. And if we can just get the band on film—millions of people will see Teenagers in Love, too. We could be famous overnight!"

I had to admit it was a good idea. For a while now we'd been looking for a break, a way to start getting some attention. And it looked to me like this movie could be a shortcut to rock stardom.

On the other hand, hadn't I just spent the whole morning trashing everybody else for letting the movie change them? I didn't want to be a hypocrite.

"Dylan? What do you say?"

"I don't know. . . ."

"Come on, man, you've got to go along with it. If you won't do it for yourself, think of me and Arseman. You'll be doing it for us. And don't forget all our fans—and the future fans who don't know about us yet. You'd be depriving a whole generation of rock fans. Nobody would get the chance to hear the Teenagers! It's practically a crime!"

"I guess you're right," I said. My doubts were fading fast. The more Chris talked it up, the better it sounded.

"Let's go for it," I said.

"All right!" Chris gave me a high five.

"There's just one problem, though," I said. "How are we going to get the band in the movie?"

"They're filming at the Avalon, right?" answered Chris. "So all we have to do is get a gig there, and we're set. I just hope they film while we're playing."

"And I hope we can get the gig," I said.

"We've got to. So, Dylan, from now on the most important thing to us is getting the band in that movie. Deal?"

"Deal." As I shook Chris's hand, I felt a little twinge of conscience. I told myself I was just doing this for the sake of the band—but was I? Or was the band just an excuse? Did I secretly want to see myself as a star?

Maybe I'm just as geeky as the rest of them, I thought. Just as big a fool as Matt, as phony as Courtney, as star-struck as Brooke . . .

Nah.

Chris went on his way. I stopped by the bathroom to check my hair in the mirror.

CHAPTER 4

Arseman

I THOUGHT MONDAY was bad, but Tuesday was even worse. When I got to school that morning, I felt as if I'd walked into another dimension and ended up on Mars. The weirdest thing of all hit me in the face as soon as I went through the door: Brooke and Dylan walking together, *holding hands*.

That's it, I thought. The world has come to an end. I mean, I never thought I'd see the day when Brooke and Dylan would get along, much less touch each other. Everybody had fallen for Brooke's little tricks at least once—everybody but Dylan. He was always the one who could see right through her.

I did a double take, just to make sure it was really Dylan and Brooke I'd seen. It was definitely Brooke, dressed as always in a chic and probably expensive outfit. And the guy with her couldn't be anyone but Dylan, in his ripped jeans and leather jacket. Neither one had changed a bit. Except that now, all of a sudden, they were an item.

Something funny is going on, I thought, and I wish I knew what it was. But I spent so long staring in amazement at the happy new couple that I was almost late for my first class. No time to hang around the lockers asking questions.

Luckily, my first class was history, with Courtney. I hoped she could tell me what was going on—if I could drag her away from the cameras long enough for her to act normal.

I got to class just in time and sat next to Courtney. As soon as Ms. Peyton, our history teacher, started talking, I wrote Courtney a note. It said:

```
Courtney,
    Did you see what I saw this morning?
Brooke and Dylan together—I  mean  really
```

gether. It can't be true, can it? Maybe it has
something to do with this movie. Everybody's
been acting weird since they started shooting, like a documentary about high school is
going to change their lives or something.

But Brooke and Dylan?! What do you think?

Arseman

I discreetly passed the note to Courtney. I
watched her while she read it. Suddenly, I noticed
she looked different—but I wasn't sure how. She
was wearing an "I Love Emily Brontë" t-shirt
and had a pencil tucked behind her ear. I looked
at her eyes, and then I realized what was different
about her. She was wearing glasses! Small, round,
silver-rimmed ones—very literary. But as far as I
knew, Courtney didn't need glasses.

She sure took her time writing back to me. At
last she passed me a note:

Dearest Arseman,
    Yes, indeed, I have noticed the phenom-
enon you mentioned in your missive this
morning. The entire school is abuzz with
talk. I saw Brooke standing by Dylan's
locker, playing with one of his chestnut
tresses. I would not say he looked as if he
were actually <u>enjoying</u> this, precisely, but
he did allow her to do it, which is something

he would not have done as recently as yesterday, I'll wager.

    I have no explanation for this as yet.
However, as soon as I know more, I'll be sure
to communicate it to you.

Fondly,

Courtney

"Fondly"? "Abuzz"? Did Courtney think the
camera could zoom in on a note?

Courtney was going to be no help, no help at
all. She was too caught up in becoming the next
great American author—or at least dressing the
part.

Courtney was gazing toward the front of the
room, but not at Ms. Peyton. She was adjusting
her new glasses and looking past the teacher, toward the supply closet. I followed her gaze—
straight to a cameraman and a camera.

I looked around the room. Courtney wasn't
the only one fixed on that camera. Everyone's
attention was riveted on it. Even Ms. Peyton's.

Man, I thought. The whole school's lost it.

Then I decided that maybe I ought to stop
watching everyone act weird and start listening to
what Ms. Peyton was saying.

"Next week we'll have a special treat: a whole
week of oral reports."

The class groaned. What makes teachers think that we *like* to do oral reports? I was going to be *so* busy, especially with the Academic Olympics coming up.

"I'm really surprised at your reaction," Ms. Peyton said. "I'd think you'd all like a chance to show off what you've learned, especially, well . . ." She paused, glancing at the camera. "*You* know why. You'll be doing your reports for a bigger audience than usual—more than just your classmates, if you know what I mean."

We knew what she meant, all right. The movie. That only made it worse. Not only did we have to do oral reports, but they'd be recorded for all time—for millions of viewers all over the country. Great.

"The subject will be the War of 1812. I'll divide the class into pairs, and each pair will study one aspect of the war and report to the rest of us on it." She went on to divide us and assign us each a day for our reports. Courtney and I volunteered to work together. I was really glad that I was going to work with Courtney. She is smart and of course we get along. I thought we'd have fun, and our report would turn out well, too.

All day at school I noticed cameras almost

everywhere I went. The entire place was filled with technicians and crew members, people running wires through the halls or carrying clipboards. All the teachers seemed edgy. I'd never seen some of them dressed as nicely as they were that day. It was obvious that most of the teachers were trying hard to look good for the movie, and they also acted differently in class. They seemed nervous, less willing to discipline us, and anxious to seem smart.

By lunchtime, things were in a frenzy. I was sitting by myself, trying to eat a cucumber sandwich and read my history book, but it was impossible to concentrate. And when Brooke showed up, it wasn't easy to eat, either.

She didn't just walk into the lunchroom; she made an entrance. "I'm here, everyone!" she announced. "Everyone" ignored her.

"You can relax, Brooke," said Amanda. "There aren't any cameras in here."

"Oh, no?" said Brooke. She went to a long curtain against the back wall and pulled it aside. There was a microphone hidden behind it.

"It may not be a camera, little sister," Brooke said haughtily. "But it's just as important—for voice-overs. You know what voice-overs are, don't you?" she continued. "That's when there's some kind of narration and the film shows different scenes. Anyway, that darling Jack Rhea doesn't want to miss a minute of my incredibly fabulous life. When the world sees this movie, they will take me to their hearts and make me the star I deserve to be."

Now you understand why I was having trouble eating.

"Brooke, you make me sick," Amanda said with up-front honesty. She left the room in disgust.

Brooke just shrugged it off. "She's jealous," she said to Stacy. "She's always been jealous of me. I try to be as understanding as I can about it."

Stacy was slouching quietly on a bench, looking nervous. Her long brown hair was hanging limply in her face, and she was wearing a white schoolgirl blouse with a baggy beige skirt. Stacy is the kind of girl who doesn't stand out in a crowd, but that's okay. Not everyone can run around in flashy clothes like Brooke. But Stacy looked up to Brooke. She followed her around, wanted to look like her, dress like her, be like her.

"Stacy, is something wrong?" Brooke sat next to Stacy and put her arm around her in that not-very-sincere way she has. "If there's anything you need, I'm always here for you."

Stacy turned her big, sad eyes to Brooke. "You've got to help me, Brooke. All these cameras make me feel so . . . well, invisible. When this movie comes out, I want to be noticed! I want to look good. Not just good—great! Like you do, Brooke."

Brooke patted her hair with one hand, smugly.

I couldn't help but put my two cents in. "I think you look fine, Stacy."

Brooke gave me a withering look. "What do you know about it, Arseman?"

"Thanks for saying that, Arseman," Stacy said quickly. "But I really do want to make a change."

I shrugged and tried to go back to my book.

"Brooke?" said Stacy. "Will you help me?"

"Of *course* I will, Stacy. You've come to *exactly* the right person." She stood up and looked Stacy over. "Now, let's see. . . . There's not much we can do about the clothes today, but we *can* put a little color in your face. I'll give you a makeover!"

Stacy's face lit up. "Thank you, Brooke! This is great!"

Brooke opened her bag and pulled out an elaborate makeup kit. "I'm going to make you so glamorous you'll draw stares wherever you go," she told Stacy.

She darkened Stacy's eyebrows, drew a thick black line around her eyes, coated her lashes with purple mascara, slathered on blush, and drew a curvy mouth on her face with bright red lipstick. By the time she was finished, Stacy looked like she was made up for Halloween.

Brooke pulled a little mirror out of her purse and handed it to Stacy, saying, "Ta da! I'll show you how I did it so you can copy it yourself and look glamorous every day!"

Stacy held up the mirror and looked. Her eyes widened in horror. "Brooke! I look terrible!"

"Stacy, how can you say that?" Brooke pretended to be deeply offended. "You look *gorgeous*."

"No, I don't," said Stacy. "This is way too much makeup." She took a tissue from her pocket and tried to rub some of it off, but it didn't help.

"Stop that, Stacy!" said Brooke. "You are so unsophisticated. Of course it looks like too much makeup now, up close and to the naked eye. But on camera, it will look great. You'll look as if you're not wearing any makeup at all!"

I looked at Stacy and shuddered. She *was*

wearing way too much makeup. I knew that actors wore makeup on camera, but this was ridiculous. No matter what Brooke said, it would never look natural.

"Trust me, Stacy," said Brooke. "Have I ever let you down?"

Yes, I thought, but I kept it to myself.

"I guess not," said Stacy. "I just hope you're right. I still think it looks funny."

Brooke was right about one thing—with all that makeup on, Stacy certainly drew stares.

When Matt and Jake walked into the lunchroom, Matt took one look at Stacy and let the basketball he was spinning on his finger bounce to the floor. Jake, a really nice guy who doesn't like to hurt people's feelings, tried to suppress his laughter.

"Stacy!" Matt said. "What's that stuff all over your face?"

Stacy looked to Brooke for reassurance. Brooke smiled and nodded at her. Stacy sat up straighter and said, "It's makeup. I know it's a little on the heavy side, but it will make me look great on film."

Jake and Matt couldn't say another word. They were shocked. They just left, shaking their heads in disbelief.

"Don't worry, Stacy," Brooke said, patting Stacy on the back. "They're just stupid boys. They'll be falling all over you after they see you in the movie."

"I hope you're right," Stacy said uncertainly.

"I'm right, I'm right. Now come on—let's get you in front of some cameras."

She steered Stacy out of the room, leaving me alone at last. Unfortunately, my appetite was completely gone by then. I ended up feeding my sandwich to the birds.

CHAPTER 5

Dylan

I WANT TO get the story straight. Okay, so maybe I made a mistake. I know there were rumors flying that week about me and Brooke. Yes, we did walk around holding hands, but only when there were people nearby who might see us. And I swear I never kissed her.

I know it sounds weird, but I was just *pretending* to be Brooke's boyfriend. Here's how it started:

I was rummaging through my locker on Monday afternoon when Brooke came up to me with that fake-o sweety-sweet smile of hers that you can see by at night. "Hi, Dylan," she said. She ran one of her fingers down the front of my shirt.

"Watch it, Brooke," I said. I know she's just a flirt.

But she wouldn't lay off. "Dylan," she said, "I think you'd better be nice to me."

"Oh, yeah?" I said. I was skeptical. "Why is that?"

"Because I need you—and you need me."

I started laughing. "I don't know why you think you need me, Brooke. But I *know* I don't need you."

"That's where you're wrong, Dylan," she said. "We need each other. And if we work together, we'll both benefit."

"I don't see how I can benefit from doing anything with you, Brooke." I started to walk away. I just didn't trust her. She's always got some scheme going.

"Dylan, wait," she said. "You've got to listen to me. I think this is something that's as important to you as it is to me."

I stopped and said, "Okay, I'll listen, but make it quick. What is it?"

"It's about the movie. . . ."

I have to admit that this did get my attention. I'd been thinking about the stupid movie ever since I'd had that talk with Chris about the band.

I couldn't think of a good way to guarantee that the band would get camera time, even if we did get a gig at the Avalon. So when Brooke mentioned the movie, I thought it wouldn't hurt to hear what she had to say. If there's one thing Brooke is good at, it's drawing attention to herself.

"What about it?"

"Well, I don't know if you knew this, but Jack Rhea just happens to be an old friend of my father's."

"Really." For all I knew, she could be making this up. But I waited to hear more.

"Yes. He had dinner at our house on Friday night. We had a fascinating conversation about his plans for the movie, and I must say he was really taken with me. He thought I was one of the most charming and interesting high-school girls he had ever met."

Sure, Brooke, you're *so* charming, I thought. But I didn't say it out loud. What if she really had put one over on Jack Rhea? Then she might be right—I really might need her.

"I made such a big impression on him, in fact, that he wants to feature me very prominently in the film. He thinks I have the potential to be a huge star. Isn't that wonderful?"

"Just great, Brooke. But what does all this have to do with me?"

"Well, Jack just *assumed* that a girl as beautiful as I am would have a boyfriend, and he really planned on featuring a teen couple in the film. I didn't have the heart to tell him that I happen to be between boyfriends at the moment—so I thought of you."

"Me? Why me?"

"Because as a couple, you and I make a great story. You know: the rebel and the rich girl."

"The who and the what?"

"Jack loved it. I've already told him all about you, and he agreed that the two of us will be the main focus of the movie."

"He said that?"

"Well, not in those exact words, but I know he's going to pay extra attention to us. So, that means you and I will have to pretend to be going out together. I'm sure that won't be too tough for you—"

"Hold on. I never said I'd do this—and I won't. I'm not going to pretend to be your boyfriend just so you can be a star."

"Dylan—"

"No way!"

"Dylan, you're forgetting something here. I'm not the only one who'll get something out of this. What about the band?"

She was right—the band. This was the perfect way to make sure we got some publicity. But I looked at Brooke, with her sprayed-on hairdo and her plastered-on smile. I would have to tell people I was going out with her. I'd have to pretend to like her in front of an audience of millions. Even supposing I was capable of doing this, was it worth it?

"If you'll just go along with this, I promise you'll get lots of time on camera. The band is part of the whole package. Jack loves the idea of the band—or at least, he thinks it's cool that I'm going out with a guy who's in a band."

"You're *not* going out with a guy who's in a band—not me, anyway. Get that straight."

"Okay, okay. But will you pretend? Will you go along with it?"

I hesitated. This wouldn't look good for me. Brooke was definitely not my type. But the band—we could really use the boost. And once the filming was over, I could go back to my normal hate-hate relationship with Brooke.

"I'll do it," I said. "But get one thing clear. I

may be *pretending* to be your boyfriend, but that's all it is—*pretending*. Don't get any ideas that I really like you or anything."

She got a hurt look on her face, just for a second. "Don't worry. I'm not so crazy about you, either. But everybody has to believe that we are really going out. If Jack finds out that we're just pretending, we'll end up on the cutting room floor—and so will the band. Got it?"

I knew it would be tough, pretending to be Brooke's boyfriend and not telling anybody the truth. People were bound to ask what was going on. But if the band got famous because of this movie, it would be worth it. Forget Brooke; I could go out with any girl I wanted! I wasn't doing it just for myself, though. The way I saw it, by going out with Brooke I was sacrificing myself for the good of the band. I sure hoped that Chris and Arseman would appreciate it. They'd *better*.

Then Brooke took my hand and said, "Well, we might as well get started."

So we walked down the hall together to our lockers. She was smiling and waving at everybody like we were part of some geeky parade or something. People stopped when they saw us and stared. They whispered behind our backs. Brooke was eating it up, but I couldn't look anyone in the eye. I knew what they were all thinking. They couldn't believe that Brooke and I were walking down the hall together, holding hands. They were wondering, "Are Brooke and Dylan dating? How did she ever get him to go out with her?" And those were questions I couldn't answer—not until the movie was over. I began to wish it were over already.

The next morning Brooke caught me as I was going into school and made me do that parade thing with her again. After that I found myself dodging questions for the rest of the day. I just didn't want to talk to anybody. Then, just before lunch, Billy came into the guys' bathroom and caught me standing in front of the mirror, combing my hair.

I usually feel a little uncomfortable around Billy as it is, ever since Chris and I kicked him out of the band. I really like Billy, but as a drummer he just wasn't good enough for the Teenagers. Even so, I hated to let him go—but Chris convinced me that the band would never improve as long as Billy was the drummer. I had no choice. I'd been avoiding Billy ever since—and I think he'd been avoiding me, too.

"Hi, Billy," I said. I stuffed my comb into my back pocket.

"Hi," Billy said sullenly. "Don't stop combing your hair on my account."

"Look, Billy—"

"Hey, if you're about to apologize to me again for kicking me out of the band, I don't want to hear it."

I tried to protest, but apparently he had something he wanted to get off his chest. "I'm glad I'm not in your stupid band," he said. "You're just as bad as all the others, selling out so you can look good in the movie. You don't really care about the music—all you care about is if your hair looks good and your clothes are cool. Well, I don't want to be in a band that's all image—I want to play music."

I was too stunned to say anything back to him. I knew he was mad at me, so I tried to think that what he said came from anger, not from the truth. I tried to believe that I didn't deserve it. Looking back on it now, I think that deep down I knew he was right. I just tried to put it out of my head, to forget about it. Things were too complicated just then to try to figure out what was going on in Billy's mind. I had to figure out my *own* mind first.

Chris came up to me at lunchtime and said,

"There are some wild rumors going down about you, Dylan. They're not true, are they?"

"I don't know what you're talking about," I said, looking away. I didn't feel safe telling him the truth. He has a big mouth, and if the movie people heard that Brooke and I were faking it, it was all over.

"Oh, no?" said Chris. "There sure is a lot of talk. One story is that Brooke is paying you to be her boyfriend. Another one says you've been in love with her since kindergarten. Either way, what it all comes down to is that you and Brooke are going out. True?"

"Mind your own business," I said angrily. I walked away. I didn't know what else to do. I couldn't deny the rumors—that would risk the movie. But I couldn't bring myself to say they were true, either. Not only was it a lie, it was also too embarrassing.

To get myself through this torture, I kept my mind on the band. That's what I was doing all this for, right?

After school I headed over to the Avalon to see about getting a gig. The place was buzzing. It seemed as if everybody I knew was there. Brooke had gone to the mall with Stacy, thank God, so I was free from her until the next day. Or so I thought.

One of the first people I saw when I walked into the Avalon was Arseman. She was on her way out. "It's too much of a scene in here," she said.

"Wait a second, Arseman," I said. "Don't leave yet. I want to talk to you." I wanted to tell her about the gig Chris and I were planning.

"Okay," she said. She went to the counter and sat on a stool. "What's up?"

I took a seat next to her and ordered a soda. "Arseman, listen—Chris had a great idea yesterday. We're going to get a gig at the Avalon if we can swing it. I'm not sure when it will be, but it has to be soon. We're going to try to get this Jack Rhea guy to film it. We figure it'll be great publicity for the band. What do you think?"

Arseman nodded. She has a pretty smile, warm brown skin, and wild, thick, curly black hair. I like Arseman. She's cool.

"So you're up for a gig?"

"Sure," she said. "I think it's a great idea. But we've got to rehearse if we're going to do it. If this gig is going to be filmed, we can't screw up. The band has to be really tight."

"Definitely," I said. My soda came, and I took a sip. Arseman was quiet for a minute. Then she said, "Uh, by the way—what's going on between you and Brooke?"

Not her, too. There was no getting away from this.

"Nothing," I said.

She stared into my eyes. I think she was trying to tell whether or not I was lying. "Nothing?" she said. "Are you sure? I saw the two of you together this morning, and you were looking pretty friendly. If that's nothing, I'd like to see your idea of something."

I started drumming my fingers on the counter. I was feeling nervous. I hate lying. And I really respect Arseman. I knew she could see right through me. I also knew she could keep a secret. So I thought, just this once, I'll get it off my chest. I had to tell *somebody* what was going on. I couldn't keep up this phony romance thing alone. Maybe if I told Arseman what I was doing, she'd tell me it was okay.

She saw that I was nervous—the finger drumming must've given me away. "Dylan?" she said. "Is something wrong?"

"I've got to tell you something, Arseman. But it's a secret. You have to promise not to tell anyone."

She leaned toward me with a serious expression and said, "What is it? I promise I won't tell a soul."

I glanced around to make sure no one was listening. The coast was clear. "It's about Brooke," I began.

"Yes—?"

"I am going out with her—but I'm not. Know what I mean?"

She looked totally confused. "Not really."

"I'm doing it for the sake of the band—I swear. Otherwise, you know I'd never go near her."

"Slow down, Dylan. *What* are you doing for the sake of the band? And what does the band have to do with Brooke?"

"Jack Rhea is friends with her father. He told her he'd feature her in the movie—her and her boyfriend. So she asked me to play the boyfriend."

Arseman stared at me. "And you said yes?" She couldn't believe it. But I figured that was just because she didn't know the whole story.

"I had to, Arseman. Don't you get it? She's going to get Jack to give us lots of time on camera—and I'm going to use that time to promote the band. It's the opportunity of a lifetime. I couldn't pass it up!"

"Dylan, she's just using you."

"I know that. But I'm using her, too. I'm getting something out of it. And so are you, and Chris, too. I'm doing it for you guys, too, you know."

She looked a little skeptical at this. "Don't do me any favors, Dylan."

"I didn't mean it that way. I just meant, well, what harm could it do? This band really means a lot to me."

"I know it does, Dylan. But is it really worth all this trouble?"

"I think it is, Arseman. Remember, don't tell anybody—not even Courtney. The whole thing will fall apart if Jack Rhea finds out we're faking it."

"I won't tell. I promise."

I looked around one more time to make sure no one was watching or listening. No one was paying any attention to us at all.

CHAPTER 6

Courtney

I SHOULD LIKE with all my heart to apologize for my recent unusual behavior. . . .

Okay, I'll cut it out. I was as caught up in Jack Rhea's documentary as anybody else. Maybe even more so. After all, this was my chance to make my dull, boring life more exciting. But how exactly? As soon as the principal told us about it, I started to wonder: How would I look on film? What sort of person was I, really? When I saw myself in the movie, would some part of my personality I'd never noticed before suddenly show up? Would it tell me something new about myself? How would all my friends see me?

I wrote this down in my diary, trying to work it all out. And then, while I was writing, it just came to me: I am a writer. I am a writer, I thought, and that's the way I want other people to see me. So I was determined to let that side of myself come out in the movie. What could be more interesting? It never occurred to me that I might look silly. In my mind, nothing a writer did could ever be silly—only poetic or romantic or inspired.

I put down my pen and studied myself in the mirror. I looked at my round face, my ordinary mouth, my curly brown hair tumbling over my shoulders in its usual messy way, and I didn't see a writer. Just a regular girl. What was missing?

Glasses! All writers wore glasses, didn't they? And even if they didn't, I was sure they'd help me look more literary. People would see me in my glasses and think, all that reading and writing every night by candlelight has ruined her eyes!

So I went to the mall and bought myself a pair of silver wire rims, with clear glass in them instead of lenses. I made the optician check my eyes out first—who knew, maybe I really did need glasses. But my eyesight turned out to be twenty-twenty.

My new glasses made me feel very inspired, so as soon as I got home I began to write. I spent the whole weekend writing. By Monday morning I had written several performance pieces. Some of them were about how I feel about my parents, who are getting divorced. I thought it would be nice to have my brother, Billy, perform them with me in front of the cameras.

Ever since my parents separated, I've lived with my mom, and Billy has lived with my dad. Billy has been having a hard time dealing with the divorce, and because we don't live together anymore, I'm not around as much for him when he needs someone to talk to, or whatever. I told myself that drawing him into these performance pieces would be a way for us to spend time together and maybe explore our feelings about the divorce at the same time. And he might begin to feel better about being kicked out of the band, too. I didn't think I was doing it for selfish reasons.

Anyway, I had ideas for some other performance pieces, too, and I thought I'd get some of my friends to help me. Ha! I talked to a few of them about it, and they all refused. I just couldn't understand it.

On Tuesday morning the first person I ran into was Stacy. I told her my plans. I had an idea for a skit about a mousy girl (based on Stacy, herself) who wants to be liked so badly that she's even willing to be friends with a vain rich girl (based on Brooke) that no one else likes. She admires this rich girl so much that she is blind to her faults. Basically, it was the story of Stacy and Brooke. Of course, I didn't tell Stacy about the "mousy" part, but I was secretly hoping that my little skit would help her see the error of her ways. You see, I really didn't get into this movie thing just to advance my writing career. I wanted to help other people with my work.

When I told Stacy about my performance idea, she acted really excited. At last, someone was willing to act out one of my pieces! "I'm so flattered you want me to star in your play," she said. "But where will it be performed?"

"All over school," I said. "In the hallways. In the gym. On the ball field. At the Avalon. It will be living theater, like performance art. I'll give you different situations, and you can act them out wherever we happen to be for whomever happens to be there at the time."

Stacy looked confused. "I don't get it," she said. "You mean, we won't be doing this on a stage?"

"No." I moved closer to her. "Look around you, Stacy," I whispered, indicating the camera operator within sight of our lockers. "There are cameras everywhere, filming us in action. Jack Rhea doesn't want to shoot a silly school play. He wants to take real life and turn it into art. So we'll make our art part of the life of the school—and he'll put it on film. Who knows, Stacy—maybe we'll both be discovered!"

Stacy looked a little nervous. Her lower lip was trembling. "I'm not so sure about this," she said. "I've never acted before. . . ."

"Don't worry," I said. "You'll be great! You don't even have to act. Just be yourself!"

Stacy still looked doubtful, but I ignored it. "We'll start right after lunch. We can do the first scene right here in the hallway, by the lockers. That's where all the action is."

She said she'd be ready. But something happened that I didn't expect. I thought we'd act out a story about a nice, plain girl like Stacy who wants to make friends but chooses the wrong people to be friends with. Apparently, that wasn't what Stacy thought we were doing. Judging from the way she looked that afternoon, she thought her character was supposed to be a girl from outer space.

I didn't even recognize her when she came in. Her face was *covered* with makeup. Where was the shy, mousy girl I had expected? She looked all wrong for the performance—wrong, wrong, wrong!

I finally recovered from my shock enough to ask, "Stacy, what happened to you?"

She gave me a bright smile and said, "Brooke gave me a makeover. Do you like it?"

"Um—well, Stacy," I stammered, "it's an awful lot of makeup."

"I know," she said. "But Brooke says you have to wear a lot of makeup when you go before the cameras. Otherwise, you just fade into the background."

I stared at her while I mulled this over. It's like life imitating art, I thought. Stacy was so insecure, she let Brooke make her over for the movie. That was exactly the kind of thing that the character in my performance piece would do. It was perfect!

"Okay, Stacy," I said. "Let's get started."

We hadn't rehearsed at all, because I wanted the performance to seem spontaneous, as if it were really happening. I was going to be the narrator. Stacy was going to play Stacy, the insecure girl. Everyone else we ran into would play themselves.

I hunted through the halls until I found a camera operator stationed by some lockers. Perfect. I positioned Stacy in front of the camera and stood next to her. "This is Stacy," I said in my deep narrator's voice. At least, I tried to make it sound deep. "She's your typical insecure high-school student. She'll do anything to be liked."

"Hey!" Stacy said, turning to face me. "That's not true!"

"Stop it, Stacy," I whispered. "You're out of character."

"What do you mean, out of character!" she said. "You told me to be myself!"

"I know that," I said. "You *are* insecure, aren't you?"

I guess that really wasn't a very tactful thing to say. Stacy got very angry.

"Speak for yourself, Miss Literary," she shot back. "Since when do you wear glasses, huh? Since yesterday!"

She'd hit a sore point there. "Stacy, these glasses are an extension of my true personality. It's just a cruel twist of fate that my eyesight happens to be perfect."

"Well, I say it's a cruel twist of fate that I ever agreed to be in your performance piece in the first place. So there!"

She marched off down the hall. I guess I misjudged her. She wasn't as insecure as I thought.

Okay, I thought, so that didn't work out. No

big deal; I've still got plenty of ideas left. In fact, maybe I could salvage this little fiasco by reading a poem I wrote over the weekend. After all, the camera was still rolling.

I pulled a sheet of paper from my notebook and began to read aloud.

" 'The Loneliness of the Young Writer,' by me, Courtney."

> *"How painful to be sensitive*
> *creative*
> *and young—reaching*
> *to the outer limits of my mind*
> *in a school full of philistines*
> *mall rats*
> *jocks. Who will understand*
> *me? Who will ever—"*

"Hi, Courtney. What are you doing?"

I stopped reading and turned to see Jake standing beside me, looking over my shoulder at the poem.

"Jake," I said, "you're interrupting me. I'm giving a poetry reading."

He glanced around and said, "For whom? There's nobody around except that woman running the camera."

"Exactly."

He gave me a look with those brown eyes of his that said, "Oh, I get it," in a not entirely flattering way. Then he waved at the camera and said, "Hi, Mom. Hi, Dad."

"Stop joking around. This is serious. Art is being created here, Jake. This is *poetry*," I said angrily.

"So-rree," Jake said, backing away from me. "It looks like I've made a terrible mistake. I thought you were my friend Courtney, but I can see you're really an art snob. Call me when Courtney comes back."

I wasn't worried—I knew Jake wouldn't stay mad at me for long. I shrugged and finished reading my poem. When it was over, I took a bow and left.

After my last class, I went looking for Billy. I wanted to talk to him about my next performance project, and I also had something I wanted to give him.

I found him sitting alone in front of his locker. He looked very unhappy.

"Hi, Billy," I said, sitting next to him. "What are you doing?"

"Nothing."

"How's Dad?"

"Fine. Just fine."

He was obviously in a bad mood, and I should have known it wasn't a good time to bring up my performance piece idea. But I was so caught up in the whole thing that I wasn't thinking straight. Besides, there was a camera rolling, and I didn't want to miss the opportunity.

"Listen, Billy," I began. "I have this great idea. I worked all weekend on some scenes to act out in front of the cameras while Jack Rhea is making his documentary. Some of them have to do with divorce, and I thought you might want to act them out with me."

Billy looked at me as if he thought I was crazy. "You're kidding, right?" he said.

"No, I'm not. This movie is a great opportunity for me to showcase my writing, and—"

Billy stood up now, furious. "The movie! That's all anybody cares about or talks about anymore. Dylan and Chris are trying to get the band into the movie, and you're trying to show off, too. I'm sick of hearing about the stupid movie!"

I stood up to try to calm him down. "Listen, Billy, be reasonable. You're just upset because things aren't going so well with Dad. You don't have to take it out on me." I pulled a book from my backpack and said, "Here, Billy. Read this. I think it will really help you."

He hesitated. Then he took the book from me and looked at it as if it were contaminated or something. "What is it?" he asked.

"It's a book, silly. A novel about a kid like you whose parents are getting divorced. Billy," I said, addressing the camera, "the answer to any problem you have can be found in a book."

He glared at me angrily and threw the book to the floor. "I don't need a book," he said. "I need a family!" Then he ran off down the hall.

"Billy!" I called. "Wait!" I started after him and crashed into Arseman.

"Courtney! Hi!" she said. "Want to get together and talk about our history project?"

"Oh, Arseman, not now," I said irritably. "I've got too many important things to worry about!"

I ran down the hall after Billy. And I never did get around to talking about that history project with Arseman.

CHAPTER 7

Brooke

THE WEEK JACK Rhea shot that movie was like heaven for me. For the first time since kindergarten, I really looked forward to going to school. I walked down the halls and into the classrooms, looking for cameras wherever I went. Every graceful, elegant move I make is being recorded for posterity, I thought happily. And with Dylan beside me, I was sure I looked even better than usual. It was fun, being around Dylan. I couldn't help thinking that he really would make a good boyfriend—a good *real* boyfriend.

Everything was going just as I'd planned. In fact, Dylan had agreed to my little scheme more quickly than I'd expected him to. Could it be, I wondered, that he likes me more than he's willing to admit?

I was whistling to myself when I got home on Tuesday afternoon. I hadn't even bothered to bring any books home from school. Who had time for homework? I could always catch up later. But now it seemed like the least important thing in the world. I had a closetful of new clothes, a great new haircut, and an adorable new boyfriend. But then, I thought, I'm practically a movie star, so I couldn't expect any less, could I?

Then Amanda had to come along and spoil my good mood.

"I saw you slobbering over Dylan all day long today," she said in her obnoxious voice. "When are you going to get the picture? He doesn't like you and he never will."

Amanda has a huge crush on Dylan herself. I laugh whenever I think about it. Imagine, Little Miss Snottypants and Dylan, just about the coolest guy in school!

"As usual, Amanda," I replied haughtily, "you are way behind the times. Haven't you heard the rumors? It's all over school, and it's true: Dylan and I are going out."

"I heard some rumors you haven't heard," she

sneered. "Nobody really believes the two of you are together. Some kids are saying you're paying him to hang around you."

This got me, I must admit. Were people really saying that? Why would they want to say such a mean thing about me? Were they jealous? That could be it.

But then, I thought, Amanda must be lying. She's just jealous.

"You can say whatever you like, Amanda," I said to her calmly. "The fact remains that Dylan is now *my* boyfriend—and not yours."

She smoldered for a few minutes. I would have kicked her out of my room, but I enjoyed watching her stew.

At last, the Bratty One spoke. "I can't wait to see this documentary, Brooke. You think you're going to come off like some kind of glamorous teen queen—but you won't. Maybe, for the first time, you'll see yourself as you really are."

I laughed in her face. "I know how I really am—fabulous. Now get out of my room. I have a phone call to make—a very *personal* call."

She stomped out, and I shut the door behind her. Then I made myself nice and comfy on my bed and dialed Dylan's number. I just happened to have it memorized.

The phone rang five times, and no one answered. I decided to let it ring a little longer. Dylan was probably out in the garage, and it would take him a long time to get to the phone. I was all ready to hang up after the fifteenth ring, when at last someone answered. It was Dylan.

"Yeah?" he said, sounding out of breath.

"Hi, Dylan. It's me." I used my low and sexy voice. It gets them every time.

He paused for a second. Then he said, "Me who?"

"Don't you recognize my voice? It's someone very near and dear to you."

"What is this? Some kind of joke?"

For some reason my sexy voice didn't seem to be working this particular time, so I dropped it. Sometimes Dylan's just a little bit thick, if you ask me. In my normal voice I said, "Dylan, it's me, Brooke. Your girlfriend?"

"Brooke, you're not my girlfriend, and you know it. Now what do you want? I'm busy."

"You are? What are you doing?"

"Well, not that it's any of your business, but Chris and I are trying out a new song for the band. We've got a lot of work to do to get ready for our gig on Tuesday."

"You've got a gig on the last day of filming! Congratulations! Where is it?"

"At the Avalon. Look, I've got to go. . . ."

So, I thought, they got a gig at the Avalon. Jack Rhea is sure to put that in the movie. "Dylan, why didn't you tell me this sooner?" I said aloud. "You know I'd want to be there to cheer you on. And besides, Jack would be sure to notice if your *girlfriend* wasn't there."

"Okay, so I'll see you there. 'Bye—"

"Dylan, wait!"

"Listen, Brooke. It's one thing to pretend to be going out while we're at school, but it's another thing to keep me on the telephone all afternoon. You're not really my girlfriend, so I don't have to talk to you. Good-bye."

How do you like that? He hung up!

I didn't let it bother me. My mind kept going back to that gig at the Avalon. I knew that Dylan was counting on it to launch the band to stardom. The Teenagers are pretty good, I thought, but they'd be a lot better if they had a more exciting lead singer. And Dylan would be grateful to that person for the rest of his life. He'd probably do anything for someone who helped his career. I couldn't stop thinking that the gig would be a perfect chance to show off my magnetism and audience appeal—not to mention my considerable talents. And it would make Dylan look at me in a new light. Jack was sure to give it a lot of screen time. If only there were some way I could be a part of it. . . .

CHAPTER 8

Arseman

"**H**EY, ARSEMAN. WHEN is a car not a car?"
"I'm sorry, John. I just don't have
time for jokes right now." I guess this was kind of
rude of me, but I couldn't help it. John was telling
jokes again. John is a short, dark-haired under-
classman who is a really nice guy. That is, he *was*
a really nice guy until the cameras started rolling.
Ever since, he'd gotten it into his head that he was
a born comedian, and he wouldn't say anything in
a normal way—all he did was tell jokes. *Bad*
jokes. At first I pretended to laugh at them, but
I couldn't pretend any longer. I was sick of going
along with everyone else's fake new identities.

Brooke and her movie star thing, Courtney and her literary thing, Dylan and his rock star thing, and now John and his comedian thing—I was ready to scream! And it didn't help that I had never been so busy in my life. I didn't have *time* to play along with everybody's little whims. I had way too much to do.

John ignored my rudeness and insisted on finishing his joke. "When is a car not a car? Give up? Okay, I'll tell you. When it turns into a parking lot! Heh heh heh."

"That's hilarious, John," I said, not laughing. I tossed my backpack over my shoulder. "You should be on TV." I ran down the hall without waiting for a response. I was late for band practice, just one of the zillion things I had to squeeze into my day. That oral history project was set for next Monday, and I couldn't get Courtney to help me with it at all. Then there were the Academic Olympics on Friday.

The Academic Olympics are kind of like a game show, where students answer questions and compete against one another for medals. Mr. Phipps asked me and Ashley, among others, to be in it. It was a bigger deal than usual this year because—you guessed it—Jack Rhea was going to film it. I figured I'd better study for it. I didn't want my grandchildren to see me look stupid when they watch the movie fifty years from now.

And then there was the band. Dylan got a gig at the Avalon for next Tuesday, on the last day of filming. He and Chris wanted to rehearse every day at lunchtime and every afternoon after school. I told them they could forget about lunchtime—after school was enough rehearsal for me.

"Okay, Arseman," said Chris. "But if you mess up during the gig, we'll know why." He was taking this even more seriously than Dylan was.

I ran all the way to Dylan's garage that day, but I was still late. I walked in and found Chris giving Dylan a hard time about Brooke.

Dylan looked as if he might explode from the tension building up inside him. He obviously hadn't told Chris what he'd told me—the real reason why he was hanging out with Brooke. He must have been afraid that Chris would blab it all over the place and ruin their chance to get the band in the movie. But I hated watching Dylan just sit there and take Chris's teasing—unable to defend himself or to tell him the truth. It was a terrible sight.

"Leave him alone, Chris," I said. "We're not

going to get any practicing done if we spend all day ragging on each other."

"Okay, okay," said Chris. "Let's jam."

We rehearsed for three hours. In spite of the little speech I'd made, Chris and Dylan spent a lot of time arguing over whether or not Dylan should take a ten-minute guitar solo in the middle of every song. At last they let me go. I raced home. I had a lot of studying to do.

By the time Friday came, I was exhausted. I passed a movie camera as I entered the school building, and I couldn't help but stick out my tongue at it. It was because of the movie that I hadn't gotten any sleep all week. The Academic Olympics were going to take place in the auditorium that afternoon, and I'd studied until midnight every night—after hours of band practice—to get ready for it.

As I headed toward my first class, I saw Erin and Lea walking ahead of me. Suddenly, they turned a corner and there was yet another cameraperson. Erin and Lea looked at each other, then ran off in the opposite direction.

"They've been doing that about once every ten minutes since Monday." I looked around and saw tall, dark-haired Matt standing next to his locker, watching me watch his sister and Lea. He was dribbling a basketball with his right hand and carrying a large, shiny silver trophy in his left.

"What does it mean?" I asked him. "Are they shy?"

Matt shrugged. "They're just excited, I guess. I don't know."

Matt tossed the basketball into the air, spun around beneath it, and caught it with one hand. "Have I ever shown you this trophy?" he asked me. Or maybe he was talking to the cameraperson standing behind me. "It's from last year's championships."

"No, I've never seen it—" I began. Matt held it up for me to look at. Dylan walked by just then, comb in hand. He leaned toward the trophy, looked into it as if it were a mirror, combed his hair with one quick swipe, and walked on.

"Hey!" Matt called after him. "Ask first next time, pretty boy!"

Next I bumped into Courtney and Ashley. Courtney was wearing a t-shirt that said "Poetry in Motion" and, of course, those new glasses. Ashley looked perfectly normal, dressed as she usually was in a neat sweater and a pair of corduroys.

"Hi, guys," I said. "Courtney, you're just the

person I'm looking for. We've really got to get moving on that history project. We're supposed to give our report on Monday!"

"Arseman," said Courtney in this weird low voice, "homework is ephemeral. Only art is eternal."

Then she launched into some kind of poem, if you want to call it that.

"We must free ourselves from the bonds of the mundane!" she cried. "Homework is bondage. Revolt, I say, revolt!" She threw her arms out dramatically to punctuate her words.

What was going on here? I looked to Ashley for help. She saw the confused look on my face and seemed to understand right away what I was going through.

"She's acting," Ashley explained, "or else she's reciting a poem. I'm not sure which."

"You just don't understand the art of avant-garde performance," Courtney said.

Ashley and I just looked at each other. Courtney had really gone off the deep end this time.

The first bell rang. "I've got to go," I said. I was somewhat dazed by all this. "I'll talk to you about the report later, Courtney."

"To quote the immortal bard," said Courtney, " 'Parting is such sweet sorrow.' "

The immortal bard? Ashley leaned close to me and whispered, "Lately I find 'parting' from Courtney kind of nice." I knew what she meant. It was good to find someone who was acting normal for a change. This movie business had only been going on for five days, but it felt like forever. I tried to remember what school used to be like—in the pre-movie era. Courtney was sweet and sincere; Matt was a nice, unassuming guy; Dylan was a rebel, not a rock star. . . . It all seemed like ages ago. I missed it.

At least Ashley hadn't lost her head. She was too busy studying to worry about the movie. She was going to be in the Academic Olympics that afternoon, too. Everyone expected her to win the gold medal easily.

"You ready for the Olympics?" I asked her as we moved through crowds of kids on our way to biology class.

She lowered her head and tucked a strand of silky blond hair behind her ear. "I'd better be ready," she said. "I've spent all week studying for them. My parents are expecting me to win again this year. My mom's baking a cake as we speak. She's planning to celebrate my victory after dinner tonight."

Man, I thought, is she under a lot of pressure.

But at least she's still the same old sensible Ashley. She was the only person I knew who hadn't turned into some kind of mutant because of this movie. I smiled at her and said, "You'll do great." I wanted to encourage her. As far as I could tell, Ashley was the last sane person at Hillside.

CHAPTER 9

Ashley

ALL WEEK LONG I tried to ignore those stupid cameras. I tried to ignore all the bizarre things the other kids were doing. I tried to ignore the way my teachers suddenly acted like college professors, trying to show off how smart they were. And I tried to forget about the fact that I wasn't getting along with Matt. Our on-again, off-again relationship was making me crazy. But that week all I thought about was the Academic Olympics, and all I did was study.

I made it all the way to Friday afternoon without getting rattled. The Olympics were supposed to start at three o'clock. Then, at 2:30, I bumped into Matt.

I mean I *literally* bumped into him. I was leaving the library, heading for the soda machine, and he was doing some kind of trick with his basketball. He didn't see me coming and backed right into me.

He started to say, "Hey, watch where you're going," before he saw who he'd bumped into. When he realized who it was, he stopped in midsentence and switched to, "Oh. Hi, Ashley."

"Hi," I said, and started to walk away. But he grabbed me by the arm.

"Wait a second," he said. "Can't I talk to you for a minute?"

I stopped. "Sure," I said impatiently. "What do you want to talk to me about?"

You have to understand that Matt and I hadn't had a normal conversation for weeks. It was as if there were some kind of barrier between us, and we couldn't get past it. I still had feelings for him, but we'd been through so much that I could hardly look at him without getting all emotional and upset.

"Nothing special," Matt said. "I just want to say hi."

"Hi." I turned to go. The Olympics started in less than half an hour.

But he pulled me back again. "What have you been doing lately?"

"Studying. Matt, I have to go—"

"How come you always have to go whenever you're talking to me?" he said. "You seem to have time to talk to other people—but no time for me."

"Matt, I'm busy. If you paid as much attention to me as you pay to your stupid basketball trophies you'd realize that I'm in the Academic Olympics. They start in twenty minutes, and if I don't win my parents are going to freak. So if you'll excuse me—"

"You know, Ashley, you've always got some reason to be uptight." He was getting angry now. "If it's not some academic thing, it's your parents or one of your committees—or all three at once. Sometimes I think you're just using them as an excuse not to talk to me."

"Thanks for that insightful analysis. I'll keep it in mind." I tried to walk away, but he still held my arm. "Let go of me!" I said angrily.

"Ashley—" He said something to me then, but I didn't hear it. I had just caught sight of something terrible. A movie camera. Rolling. Filming my private fight with Matt for the whole world to see. The camera operator was pointing it right at me.

It was too much. Tears welled up in my eyes. I couldn't help it.

"Ashley!" Matt said. "Ashley, are you listening to me?"

"Yeah," I answered. "And so is everybody else." I ran down the hallway and into the girls' bathroom. I was really shaken up. There was something about those movie cameras that rattled me. I'd managed to shut them out all week long and just concentrate on studying—but now it was as if they'd invaded my brain. I thought I saw cameras everywhere, and each camera was just waiting to catch me in the act of doing or saying something stupid. I felt as if this movie was being filmed just to prove to everybody that I wasn't as smart and together as they thought I was—that I was a fake.

I thought I'd be safe when I ran into the bathroom. But there, standing in front of the mirror, was the last person in the world I wanted to see after Matt. Brooke.

When I burst through the door, she turned to see who it was. I tried to hide how I felt, but she saw the tears in my eyes. She immediately put down the makeup she'd been applying and ran over to me, full of false sympathy.

"Why, Ashley!" she cried. "What in the world is wrong?"

"Nothing," I said. "Leave me alone."

She peered into my face. I turned away.

"Oh," she said. "I bet I know what it is. Jack Rhea has been shooting this movie for a week now, and I've taken up all your camera time. That's it, isn't it?"

"No, Brooke. That's not it."

She clapped her hands. "Of *course* it is. It makes perfect sense. Oh, Ashley, I'm so sorry, but we can't all be stars, you know. You have to have that little something extra—"

"Brooke, I don't care one bit about the stupid movie."

"Come now, of course you do. Everybody cares about it. It's become a part of our lives, hasn't it?" She stopped talking for a minute to look me over. "If it's not the movie you're upset about, maybe it's Dylan?"

"Dylan? What about him?"

"Don't play innocent, Ashley. I know you've had your eye on Dylan for quite some time. But he's a special guy. He needs a very special girl. Most girls just aren't good enough for him."

I'd spent so much time buried in my books that I hadn't heard the gossip about Brooke and Dylan. I had seen them together once or twice, but I hadn't thought anything of it. I thought she was just hanging around, annoying him. Now I was beginning to put two and two together. It wasn't easy to believe, though. Brooke and Dylan? It seemed like an impossible combination.

"Brooke, I don't care who you're going out with, or who Dylan is seeing. I just need to be alone for a minute, okay?"

"Sure, Ashley. Sure. I know you're burning up with jealousy. I'll leave you alone so you can stew." She picked up her purse and flounced out of the girls' room.

I glanced down at my watch, and to my horror I saw that it was five minutes to three. I wouldn't have time to be alone and collect myself. I was about to be late for the Academic Olympics.

I ran out of the bathroom, through the hallway, and down the stairs. Then I raced down another hallway until I finally reached the auditorium. I burst through the doors. There was a big audience of kids, and up on the stage were Mr.

Phipps, the other seven contestants, and my empty seat.

I ran down the aisle and up onto the stage. "Here I am," I said breathlessly. Mr. Phipps smiled at me. "Glad you could make it, Ashley," he said. "Please take your seat. I was just giving the other contestants their last-minute instructions."

I sat next to Arseman. Everybody was arranged as a panel behind a long table, facing the audience. Mr. Phipps would be at the podium just to the side of us. He was standing in front of us now.

"The camera is right there," he said, pointing to a spot in front of the stage, center. I was so nervous, I almost laughed out loud. I mean, how could we miss it? There was a cameraman and a movie camera with a red light on top about three feet away. "When the red light goes on," explained Mr. Phipps, "that means the camera is rolling. It will probably be on during the entire Olympics. You may wish to look toward the camera when you answer questions."

I stared at the camera. It looked just like the camera that had recorded my argument with Matt. It was the camera that was going to show everyone I was a big fake. Jack Rhea was going to include the Academic Olympics in his movie. My teachers would watch it. So would my parents. And all my friends. They would watch the movie over and over again, shaking their heads. "It's such a shame," they'd say. "We always thought Ashley was so smart."

Mr. Phipps went and stood behind the podium. The red light went on.

"Okay," he said. "Welcome to the Hillside Academic Olympics. Our contestants will now introduce themselves."

The kids in the audience clapped as everyone said his or her name. I barely heard the names *or* the clapping. Then it was my turn. "A-a . . ." Nothing really came out. I couldn't take my eyes off that camera. I was hypnotized by it. Finally Arseman spoke up. "Ashley," she said, and everyone laughed.

I stared at the camera. I could vaguely hear Mr. Phipps going on about the rules, but the only thought going through my mind was: I've got to win the gold. I've got to win the gold. But how? I couldn't even say my *name* into the microphone.

"Okay, first question: World War II took place during what years?"

I know that, I thought. I just studied World

War II last night. What is it? What is it? My mind wouldn't come up with the right answer.

Mr. Phipps said, "Arseman?"

"1939 to 1945," said Arseman.

Of course, I thought. You idiot!

"That is correct. Next question: Define 'osmosis.'"

Osmosis, I thought. I know that one! Come on, brain. Think!

"Brian?"

"Osmosis is when a fluid passes through a semipermeable membrane," answered a senior named Brian.

"Good. One point for Brian. Question number three . . ."

The Olympics went on and on this way. Mr. Phipps kept asking questions. I knew the answers to almost all of them—but they were stuck somewhere in the back of my brain, and no matter what I did I couldn't seem to get to them. After a while I just stopped trying.

During a break in the contest, Arseman leaned over to me and whispered, "Ashley? Are you all right?"

I nodded, my eyes still fixed on the camera.

"Why aren't you answering any questions?" she asked. "You know all this stuff."

I dragged my hypnotized eyes away from the camera and looked at her sadly. "I can't," I whispered back. "I just can't."

An hour later the Academic Olympics were finally over. Brian won the gold medal. Arseman won the silver, and a freshman won the bronze. I came in eighth, and last. I hadn't answered a single question.

CHAPTER 10

Courtney

AFTER THE FIASCO with Stacy, I gave up on my performance-art pieces. I decided to concentrate more on my poetry, because I could write it and perform it by myself. Soon I was consumed by it—poetry became my passion. I spent all week reading, writing, and reciting poetry. When the weekend came along, I shut myself up in my room and did nothing but write. I asked Mom to leave my meals outside my door, because I was in the throes of creative passion and didn't want to be interrupted for mere earthly sustenance. I also told Mom that I wasn't taking any phone calls. I was not to be disturbed.

Still, while I was busy being a poet, I had a nagging feeling that there was something else I was supposed to be doing. Was it something for Mom? Something for school? Didn't I have some kind of deadline on Monday?

Nothing came to mind. Whatever it is, I figured, it must not be very important—certainly not as important as expressing one's true emotions in words.

I went to school Monday morning with a beautiful new poem in hand. I had written it for Billy. I had tried to imagine how he felt about the divorce and wrote it down. I planned to find him, put him in front of a camera, and have him read it out loud.

This is it, I thought as I walked into school looking for Billy. This is the poem that will make my reputation across the country.

I found Billy at his locker. Luckily, there were a couple of camerapeople filming right there in the hallway. I didn't even have to go looking for them.

"Hi, Billy," I said, handing him the poem. "Here. I wrote this for you. It's called 'My Name is Billy and My Parents Are Getting Divorced.' Why don't you read it out loud?"

Billy read the poem to himself. I saw his hands

shaking. I thought it must be because he was so moved by my words. I was wrong.

He threw the poem on the floor.

"What are you doing?" I cried. How could he just toss my work away like that?

"I don't need you to tell me how to feel, Courtney," he said angrily. "I know exactly how I feel, and I can tell you all about it in my own words."

I was so surprised, I couldn't say a thing. I just stood there and stared at him. A small group of people had gathered around to see what was going on. Billy was so upset, he didn't care who heard him; he just had to talk.

"You want to know how I feel, Courtney? I feel like nobody in this whole school cares about anything but this movie! Nobody really cares about anyone else's feelings, or about what's real and true. All they want is to be movie stars! Stacy, Brooke, Matt and that stupid basketball . . . even Dylan and Chris will do anything it takes to get the band into the movie. They're more worried about how the band *looks* than how it sounds. And even you, Courtney, my own sister—all you care about is using me to help you become a famous writer. You don't even want to hear how I feel. You want me to read how you *think* I should feel! Well, I've had it! If you don't really want to talk to me, to help me, then why should I help you? You can take your stupid poems and throw them in the trash for all I care!"

He stomped off down the hall and out of the building. All I could do was watch him walk away. I was stunned. I had no idea all that was going on in Billy's mind. And I didn't know what to do about it. What a way to start the day! I felt terrible.

The bell rang. It was time for my first class—history. Arseman was in my history class. She is the most sensible person I know. I'll talk to Arseman about this, I thought. Maybe she'll help me figure out what to do.

But when I sat down next to Arseman in class, she glared at me. I was shocked. Had I done something wrong?

"Where were you all weekend?" she whispered.

"I was at home, writing. I told Mom not to interrupt me for anything. . . ."

"Courtney," said Arseman. "Have you forgotten something?"

I thought for a minute. "You know, all weekend I had this feeling that I was forgetting about something, but I couldn't think of what it was."

"I'll tell you what it was," said Arseman. "It was our oral report on the War of 1812."

Oh, no. "Whoops," I said.

I looked toward the front of the room, behind Ms. Peyton, where the camera usually was. It wasn't there. I began to feel hopeful. Maybe Arseman was mistaken. Maybe we wouldn't have to give our report today. And even if we did—maybe Jack Rhea forgot all about it. At least our oral report wouldn't be filmed—I thought.

Then Ms. Peyton said, "Well, class, it's time to begin our oral reports. Our first team is Arseman and Courtney. Girls?"

Nervously I got up from my seat. How did I get myself into this? I wondered. I always did my homework. I wasn't the type to blow off an oral report. But I hadn't prepared a single thing for this presentation. What was I going to do?

We stood in front of the class. Ms. Peyton and the other kids watched us expectantly. I looked toward the back of the room—and then I realized why I hadn't seen a camera in the front. They were filming from the back of the classroom that day—probably just so they could get a good shot of us doing our report.

Arseman cleared her throat. "Well," she

began, "our focus is on what life was like in the United States when the War of 1812 began. The fourth president, James Madison, was in the White House, and his wife Dolley . . ."

Arseman talked on and on about Dolley Madison and what people were doing in Washington. I just stood there and listened, amazed. I felt terrible. Arseman had done this entire project by herself. I didn't help her one tiny bit.

About halfway through, Ms. Peyton interrupted Arseman. "I can see you've done a wonderful job, Arseman, but I think we'd better let Courtney tell us what she's learned. Courtney?"

I looked at Arseman, and Arseman looked at me. She felt sorry for me, I could tell. She could probably see how nervous I was by the way my chin was trembling.

"Um, Ms. Peyton—" I began. I was going to admit that I hadn't done any work, that I hadn't prepared at all. That I didn't know the first thing about the War of 1812. But Arseman interrupted me.

"Actually, Ms. Peyton," she said, "Courtney and I researched this and wrote it together, but we decided it would be easier if just one of us gave the report."

I smiled weakly and tried to say, "thank you,"

to Arseman with my eyes. I think she got the message.

Ms. Peyton frowned. "Well, okay. Because this is the first report, I guess you might not have understood the assignment. I really wanted each of you to give part of the presentation."

Ms. Peyton was being unusually understanding, it seemed to me. And then I realized why. She didn't want to look mean in the movie!

CHAPTER 11

Brooke

Monday afternoon. Filming was going to end on Tuesday. And I didn't feel I'd had enough exposure. I'd hardly set eyes on Jack Rhea since he'd had dinner at our house more than a week before. Where *was* he? He never seemed to be around when I had Dylan with me. I supposed he had filmed us secretly or something. Still, I didn't feel comfortable about the way things had gone. I decided not to let Dylan out of my sight for the rest of the day, if I could help it.

I caught him leaving school that afternoon. "Oh, Dylan!" I called. "Dylan, darling! Wait up!"

He stopped, but he was scowling at me. "Don't call me 'darling,' " he growled.

I ignored him and took his arm. We started walking down the street together. "Did you hear about Billy's tantrum today? That boy is *such* a child. I heard that . . ."

Dylan suddenly stopped short. "What's the matter, dearest?" I asked him.

"Do you have to be so mean about it—enjoying other people's problems that way? And don't call me 'dearest.' " He stalked off down the street, leaving me standing there.

"Dylan! Wait!" I chased after him. I thought I knew what the *real* problem was. I wasn't talking about things that interested *him* enough. You have to do that with boys, you know—talk about sports and stuff they like. They just won't listen to any other kind of talk. So I changed the subject.

"How are things going with the band?" I asked him. "All ready for your big gig?"

"I guess so."

"Does Jack know about it? You ought to make sure he'll be there, or at least one of his crew."

"I don't think he knows," Dylan said. "I haven't seen him around lately to tell him. To be honest, Brooke, I'm not sure he knows who I am."

"Don't be silly, Dylan. Of course he knows who you are. You're my boyfriend!"

"That's not exactly how I want people to remember me," said Dylan. The guy really has no sensitivity when it comes to other people's feelings. "I also happen to be the lead guitarist for Teenagers in Love."

The band. Always harping on the stupid band. "Don't worry, Dylan. I'm sure he knows you're in a band. I'll try to find him, and I'll make sure he personally shows up at your gig. I promise. Okay?"

"Yeah. Sure. Look, I have to go practice now."

"See you later, Sugar," I said, playfully touching the tip of his nose.

I decided to head over to the Avalon to see what was going on. Stacy was sitting at the counter, and I joined her. She had tried to copy the makeup job I'd done on her, with disastrous results. Without my professional touch, she looked like a freak.

"Did you hear about the gig tomorrow?" Stacy asked by way of small talk.

"Of course," I replied sharply. "I'm Dylan's girlfriend. I know everything about him."

"Then you know Jack Rhea is going to be here to direct the camera crew himself."

I raised my eyebrows in surprise, then lowered them quickly so Stacy wouldn't see that, as a matter of fact, I hadn't known that little tidbit. I'm sure she didn't notice—she's terribly dense sometimes.

I had to say something, so I said the best thing I could think of: "Jack told me all about it himself. He thinks it will be the highlight of the movie."

Then something struck me. It probably *would* be the highlight of the movie. And I still hadn't come up with a way to be in it. Suddenly it hit me. The perfect idea. It was so simple, so fool-proof, that I couldn't believe I hadn't thought of it sooner.

"Come on, Stacy. Let's go to the mall," I said, pulling her to her feet. "We've got some shopping to do."

I dressed normally for school the next morning, but I took the brand-new sea green sequined mini dress I had bought the night before in an overnight case. I could hardly wait for the day to end. School was a madhouse because it was Jack

Rhea's final day of filming, and everybody wanted to get in their last shots at movie stardom.

It was just before last period. Time to set my plan into motion. First I had to find Dylan. The gig would begin after school, and I wanted to make sure he and Chris left to prepare for it before classes were over. Timing was crucial to my plan.

I scoured the halls looking for Dylan. Just my luck, the first person I ran into was that moron John.

"Knock knock," he said.

I ignored him.

"Hey!" he persisted, blocking my path. "I said 'Knock knock.' "

"I know," I said. "And I ignored you."

I continued on my way. At last I spotted Dylan talking to Chris by the soda machine. Perfect.

"Hi, boys," I said. "You'd better get over to the Avalon right now and set up before it gets too crowded. I heard people are cutting last period to get good seats."

"She's right," said Chris. "Let's get over there."

"Wait a second," said Dylan. "We've got to find Arseman first."

He was playing right into my hands.

"I'll find her for you," I said in my most cooperative voice. "You two just get going. You've got to have everything ready before school lets out." They were so nervous about their gig, they didn't even notice that I was being unusually helpful.

"Yeah. Thanks, Brooke," Dylan said. He and Chris went to their lockers to get their stuff and then left for the Avalon.

Now to find Arseman.

I bumped into Courtney. "Hello, Brooke," she said.

"Hi. Listen—do you know where Arseman is? It's important."

"Oh, Arseman, Arseman. Wherefore art thou, Arseman?"

Oh, brother. "Courtney, would you please talk normally for a minute?"

She looked sheepish—and rightly so. "Sorry. I think she has study hall this period."

"Great. Thanks." I ran off to the library.

I found Arseman studying at a table in a corner. I walked over and sat down beside her. "Arseman," I whispered. "Dylan sent me to give you an important message."

She looked up from her book.

"Jerry just canceled the gig. Dylan doesn't know why."

Arseman looked shocked. "That's terrible!" she whispered. "Dylan and Chris must be crushed."

"Oh, they *are*," I said in as sympathetic a tone as I could muster while whispering. "They're just *devastated*. But there's a chance the gig will be rescheduled for tomorrow. Dylan's hoping Jack Rhea will stay on to film it then."

Arseman shut her book. "I'd better go over to the Avalon and see what's happening." She started to stand up, but I pressed my hand firmly on her shoulder, forcing her to stay seated.

"No, don't do that," I said. It was really becoming a struggle to keep my voice down. Out of the corner of my eye, I saw Mr. Vogel, the librarian, look up at me.

Arseman was confused. "Why not? I'm sure I can get permission to leave study hall a little early."

"That's not what I mean," I said. "It's just that, well, Dylan is going to the garage first, and he wants you to meet him there. He told me to tell you to wait for him if you get there first."

"Oh," said Arseman. "All right."

"Don't forget—go to the garage right after

school," I said, patting her on the back. "I've got to run. See you."

I dashed out of the library to my locker. I took my overnight bag into the girls' bathroom and changed into my fabulous sequined dress. Then I hurried to the Avalon as fast as I could.

Dylan and Chris were just about set up when I got there. I checked the back of the room and was glad to see Jack Rhea and two crew members setting up their equipment. This was going to be great!

"Where's Arseman?" Dylan asked nervously. "What's taking her so long?"

"Oh, Dylan," I said sympathetically. "You won't believe this. I went to tell her to hurry on over here, but she wouldn't come."

"What?!"

"Listen," I said, taking his arm and pulling him into a corner so we could speak privately. "She's been afraid to tell you this, but she's got camera fright. She's too shy to sing in the movie."

Dylan looked at me with skepticism. He usually didn't believe a thing I said. But I was determined that he was going to believe me this time.

"That doesn't sound like Arseman," he said. "She's never been shy."

"Well, Dylan, she does put up a good front. But you don't know her as well as I do. I think all the pressure—you know, with this movie business and everything—has really gotten to her."

I watched his face carefully to see whether or not he'd buy it. He knit his brows in frustration. He was buying it, all right.

He stepped away from me and angrily stamped his foot on the floor. "How could she do this to me?" he cried.

"Dylan!" I said, taking his arm again. "Calm down. She knew this would be a big inconvenience to you, and she didn't want to let you down. That's why she asked *me* to take her place today."

Dylan stared at me in shock. "You?" he cried. I think he was getting hysterical. "*You?*" He threw his head back and began to laugh like a madman.

"Yes, me," I said indignantly. "What's so funny about that?"

"Can you sing?"

I gazed up into his eyes and said, "Can lions roar? Can monkeys swing from trees? Can Mr. Phipps bore you to tears?"

He took that to mean I could sing.

"Besides," I added, "it's perfect for our little plan. It makes a much better story if the lead singer and the lead guitarist are dating. If I'm your lead singer instead of Arseman, Jack is sure to pay extra-close attention."

Dylan sighed. "Okay, you're in. But after today, our so-called 'relationship' is over. Got it?"

"Of course, Dylan." What he doesn't know, I thought, is that after today he'll want me to be his lead singer so badly he'll never want to break it off!

Dylan broke the news to Chris, who cursed and then snarled at me. "We haven't rehearsed with her or anything!" he said angrily.

The Avalon was filling up; kids were waiting in line outside to get in and see the band. Jack Rhea came up to us and said, "Okay, are you guys almost ready to start?"

Dylan nodded, and Jack went back to his cameras. Chris said, "I guess we don't have any choice. But I'm going to kill Arseman for this."

"Don't worry, Chris," I said. "I'll be so great, you'll thank Arseman for chickening out."

I was very disappointed that neither of them mentioned my outfit. I looked much more like a rock star than Arseman ever did. But I didn't have time to fuss over it. Dylan and Chris began to tune their guitars. Dylan handed me a microphone and said, "Here. Sing into this."

"Oh," I said, taking the mike from him. "Thanks."

"The first song is 'Mama Says Be Glad.' You know it?"

"Sure." I must have heard Arseman sing that song a million times. I thought I knew the words, or at least most of them. . . .

The audience settled down, and Dylan said, "Hi, thanks for coming. We're Teenagers in Love. Well, let's begin."

He nodded to Chris, and they started to play. I wiggled my hips to the beat. I wished I could see how the sequins on my dress must have sparkled under that light.

Whoops. It was time for me to start singing.

"Well, Mama says be glad
Da da da da da da da . . ."

I kind of forgot the words to that part.

"Because I'm fifteen,
And that's a difficult age.
Da da da da da da da—
Just like a rat in a cage."

I looked back at Dylan to see how I was doing. He was frowning severely. Then I looked back at the audience and wiggled my hips some more. They started booing! I couldn't believe it! I was doing my best! I was giving it all I had. How dare they boo at me!

Chris and Dylan stopped playing. The audience was really rowdy now, making a lot of noise. Of course Roxanne, that little heavy metal head, was shouting louder than anyone. Everybody knows she'd give her right arm to sing with Chris, so that was understandable. But I saw some of my very own friends in that audience booing away like crazy.

John threw a wadded-up ball of paper at me. "Hey!" I shouted. "I'd like to see you get up and do this! At least I sing better than you tell jokes!"

Dylan took the mike away from me. "Brooke," he muttered furiously, "you're terrible. You don't even know the words. You ruined our gig, and I never want to see you or speak to you again. Now get off this stage!"

My jaw dropped down to my toes. I was tempted, very tempted, to cover my face and run off the stage. This gig had not turned out the way I'd planned—not at all. But if I ran away just then, my movie career would have been ruined.

No, I thought, I can't let that happen. There must be some way to salvage this. Then I realized

105

what had happened. I was great, I thought. So great that these unsophisticated oafs don't even know it. Well, all right. Maybe they don't recognize singing talent. But they can't deny *acting* talent!

The way I saw it, the cameras were still rolling. As far as all the people out there in TV-land knew, Dylan was my boyfriend. Here he was, breaking up with me onstage. It wasn't my ideal set-up, but it *was* a dramatic moment. Brooke, I told myself, here's your chance to show what you can do. Go for it, girl.

I took the mike back from Dylan. He was so surprised by this that he didn't struggle. "Dylan!" I wailed into the mike. "Are you breaking up with me? After all we've been through together?"

He looked a little confused. "Yes, I'm breaking up with you," he said. His tone of voice wasn't as firm as it had been before. I guess he wasn't sure what was happening—especially since I'd stuck the mike in his face to be sure to amplify his answer.

I put my wrist to my forehead and closed my eyes dramatically. "Oh, Dylan, Dylan," I moaned. "All those songs you wrote for me. The way you stroked my hair. You are my light, my life. If you leave me, I'll die. What will I do? Where will I go?"

Wait until they see this in Hollywood, I thought. They'll fall all over themselves trying to be the first to offer me a contract!

Chris tried to spoil everything by saying, "Brooke, would you just get off the stage?"

Just then, from the back of the room, a voice shouted, "Hey! What's going on here?"

It was Arseman.

"Arseman!" cried Dylan. "Thank God. Get up here and sing!"

She ran up on stage. I played it up for all it was worth.

"So!" I cried. "This is all because of *Arseman*? You're going to drop me for her? You would give up my beauty, my taste, my charm—for her?"

Arseman stared daggers at me. "You told me the gig was canceled!" she said.

"What!" Dylan and Chris were fuming.

The audience was booing more noisily than ever. Chris pushed me off the stage. I'd had enough. I ran to the back and toward the door. On my way out, though, I noticed that Jack Rhea and his crew were packing up their equipment.

Good, I thought to myself. At least they got me on film—and they won't get Arseman.

Dylan noticed that they were leaving, too. He ran back to them and said, "Mr. Rhea, please wait. There's been a big mix-up. Our real lead singer is here now, and we're ready to play the gig—the real gig. I promise you, we'll be great!"

I stood by the door, anxiously waiting to hear what Jack would say. He looked at Dylan and said, "I'm sorry, kid. I'd really love to shoot the gig—but we're out of film."

The kids in the audience called out, "Play anyway! We want to hear you!"

As I left the Avalon, Teenagers in Love began to play. I heard Arseman singing, and I had to admit she wasn't bad. But I couldn't help feeling glad that they wouldn't make it into the movie—not without me.

CHAPTER 12

Arseman

THE DAY AFTER that disastrous gig at the Avalon, everything at Hillside should have gone back to normal. The cameras were gone, the director and his crew were gone—but the tension wasn't gone.

Everyone knew that Jack Rhea was going to put together a quick rough cut of the documentary and bring it to school to show it to us in a couple of weeks. We were all a little nervous about how it would turn out. How would we come off in the movie? Even the teachers seemed nervous. And everyone kept up his or her movie personas, even though there were no cameras around to record them. Dylan still checked himself out in mirrors to make sure his hair was perfect, and John was still telling corny jokes. Matt still clung to his basketball, and Stacy still put on a ton of makeup every morning. People were used to seeing her that way by now.

Ashley had gotten over the Academic Olympics disaster pretty well—her parents gave her the cake even though she hadn't won, saying it was an honor just to be chosen to participate. But she was terrified of how that scene would look in the movie. She knew she had frozen up, and she was afraid she would look dumb in front of the whole school.

Courtney was still wearing her glasses, but she had something else on her mind besides writing. She told me she was really worried about Billy. He was avoiding her, and she didn't know what to say to him. She felt she had let him down, but she couldn't bring herself to approach him. She was afraid he hated her.

The only person who didn't seem to be the least bit nervous—about anything—was Brooke. She still acted like a movie star, getting overdressed for school every day, constantly primping in front of mirrors, and generally giving everyone the impression that she wouldn't be around much longer because Hollywood beckoned.

She didn't seem the slightest bit embarrassed about the scene at the Avalon and her big "breakup" with Dylan. As a matter of fact, I did wonder why Dylan never told anyone else about the arrangement. I guess it would just have been too humiliating for him to admit what had happened.

Anyway, the week crawled by, with everyone wondering when we'd get to see the rough cut. Finally one afternoon Courtney ran up to me and said, "I saw him! He's here!"

"Who's here?" I asked.

"Jack Rhea. I saw him in Mr. Phipps's office. Today must be the day!"

Word spread quickly. By the time Mr. Phipps called us all to an assembly, half the school was already in the auditorium, waiting for the movie to begin. Courtney, who was sitting next to me, clutched my arm nervously.

Mr. Phipps stood behind the podium, smiled at us, and cleared his throat. "This is the moment we've all been waiting for. I'm sure you're as excited as I am. Mr. Rhea has made a serious documentary about what life is really like for high-school students. He told me that at first he was thinking about concentrating on just one couple." I noticed Brooke breathe in sharply, and look at Dylan. "But then he decided to focus on the entire student body . . . and he tells me that you all were wonderful." Now Dylan was staring daggers at Brooke.

"So, without further ado . . . Rrrroll 'em!"

First there was an outdoor shot of the school building, with a title reading, "Hillside Live!" A narrator's voice said, "What happens when you mix a camera crew with a school full of teenagers? How much of what comes out on film reflects the *real* lives of the kids—and how much is just what they *want* you to see? Is it possible for high-school students to be themselves when there's a camera around? We went to Hillside High to find out."

The camera cut to the halls of Hillside. The first person we saw was John. Everybody clapped and whistled.

John stared straight into the camera and started his schtick. "Guy goes to the doctor. He says, 'Doctor, you gotta help me.' The doctor says, 'What's the matter?' The guy says, 'My wife thinks she's a chicken.' Doctor says, 'Bring her in, I'll take a look at her, I'll convince her she's not a chicken.' The guy says, 'I can't. I need the eggs.' "

We'd all heard that joke one too many times. There was good-natured hissing in the auditorium. John shrugged and said, "What? That's not funny?"

We didn't have time to dwell on John, though. Next there were shots of a volleyball game, and then some footage of Ellen, a junior who's the star of the gymnastics team. Lea and Erin were shown sitting in English class, whispering and laughing every time they looked toward the camera—and not listening to a word their teacher was saying. There was Roxanne, dancing through the halls with her Walkman on, oblivious to everyone around her. One scene showed Jake in the art studio painting at an easel, concentrating so hard that he wasn't even aware of the camera operator.

Suddenly there was a close-up of Courtney's face, glasses and all. From the corner of my eye I could see her slipping down slightly in her seat. She gripped my arm even more tightly. "This is it," she whispered.

The camera pulled away a little, and on the screen Courtney began to recite one of her poems.

With a serious expression on her face, she said:

> *"They serve us brussels sprouts*
> *in the cafeteria.*
> *What does it mean?*
> *No one likes them.*
> *What does it mean?*
> *They make us sick.*
> *What, I ask you, what*
> *do these sprouts of brussels mean?"*

Everybody laughed, and the real Courtney hid her face behind her hands.

But there was more of Courtney to come. The next scene showed her giving Billy a poem to read. The auditorium grew quiet as we watched him throw down the piece of paper and tell Courtney how angry he was, how fake everybody was acting. Billy was saying exactly what the rest of the movie was showing. When his speech was over, you could have heard a pin drop.

Courtney took off her glasses and wiped her eyes. "I've got to find Billy as soon as this is over," she said. "I can't believe I let my literary ambitions come between us." Then she handed the glasses to me and whispered, "Don't let me put these on again—unless my eyesight goes bad, of course."

The auditorium wasn't quiet for long. Dylan and Brooke were next. They were walking into the Avalon together, and Brooke was pinching Dylan's cheek and saying, "Sweet, darling Dylan! I'll bet you were just adorable when you were a baby!"

This caused screams of laughter. Tough Dylan putting up with that from Brooke! It was almost too much to bear.

I looked over at Dylan. He shrugged and rolled his eyes. He wasn't the first one people had laughed at that afternoon—and he wouldn't be the last. Everybody was getting the treatment.

It was my turn next. I was shown sitting at the counter in the Avalon. Dylan came and sat next to me. We started talking. Dylan said, "I've got to tell you something, Arseman. But it's a secret. You have to promise not to tell anyone."

Oh, no, I thought. They didn't film this—did they? The Avalon was so crowded that day, I guess I hadn't noticed any cameras.

Some kids in the audience went, "Whoooaaa." They knew this was going to be juicy. I glanced at

Brooke, who was sitting one row ahead of me. She was squirming in her seat.

That whole conversation with Dylan—the one about how Brooke got him to pretend to be her boyfriend—was played out in front of the entire school. I couldn't believe it.

The auditorium was practically in an uproar now. I sank into my seat. I hadn't told anyone Dylan's secret, but the whole school knew about it now. I looked over at Dylan; he was actually grinning! Then I understood. Brooke's scheme hadn't worked anyway, and now no one would think he'd ever liked her.

More scenes were shown: Straight interviews with people, including one with me. I hadn't even realized Brooke was edging her way into the shot! There was Ashley blowing the Academic Olympics, Matt accidentally hitting Mr. Phipps in the stomach with his basketball, teachers showing off, people saying stupid things in class . . . We were all howling with laughter. But there were also some touching moments, like Ashley and Matt hugging and making up from their fight, Roxanne looking wistfully at Chris . . .

Then came the climactic scene—the gig at the Avalon. Dylan and Chris started playing their guitars, and Brooke stood up there in that gaudy dress, trying to sing "Mama Says Be Glad" without knowing the words. It was a riot! Definitely the funniest scene in the whole movie. And then the breakup with Dylan—my stomach hurt, I was laughing so hard. But a little voice inside me wondered, how is Brooke taking this? I looked and saw that she was the only one not laughing. She was sitting quietly with her head in her hands. From the back I could tell that her ears were bright red.

I couldn't help but feel sorry for her. Crazy as it seemed, she had really thought this movie would make her a star. And even though she'd pulled such a dirty trick on me, telling me the gig was canceled and everything, I couldn't stay mad at her. I was secretly glad Jack had run out of film before I sang with the band—what if I'd come off looking as silly as Brooke?

The movie ended, and the lights came on. Everybody clapped, still laughing at themselves and at each other. Right away Stacy excused herself to go to the bathroom and wash all that goo off her face. Then Courtney said, "I can't believe I really talked that way! How did you guys ever put up with me?"

"We were too busy being jerks ourselves," Matt told her. "Me and that stupid basketball."

Courtney suddenly caught sight of Billy walking down the auditorium aisle, and she reached out to stop him. "Hey," she said quietly. "We need to talk."

He looked up at her and smiled a little. I couldn't help smiling, too. I think Courtney saw a side of Billy in that movie that she'd never really noticed before—a side that she liked and respected.

"I'll see you later, Courtney," I said, and I left her alone with her brother.

People filed out of the auditorium, laughing. I was one of the last to leave. I looked back and saw Courtney and Billy standing in a corner by the stage, talking. And sitting quietly, still in her seat, was Brooke.

I've got to say something to her, I thought. Something to make her feel better about this. But what?

I saw her lift her head and blink. I went back into the auditorium and said, "Hi, Brooke."

She smiled at me. I was surprised. "Hi, Arseman," she said. "How did you like the movie?"

I fumbled for the right thing to say. "Well, it sure made a lot of people look silly—" I began.

"It sure did," said Brooke. She seemed to be thinking about something. "You know, Arseman, this documentary has been a real revelation to me."

"It has?" Wow, I thought. Is it possible she actually learned something from this? Could there be a new Brooke in the works—a smarter, kinder, more understanding Brooke who did more than just try to grab all the attention for herself?

"Yes, Arseman," Brooke said. "It certainly has. Did you see how hard everyone was laughing when I was on-screen?"

Now I really felt uncomfortable. "Well, Brooke, they weren't really laughing *at* you . . ."

"I know that," said Brooke, musing. "All this time I've been trying to show off my dramatic talents, and I've completely ignored the obvious."

"The obvious? What do you mean?"

"I have a real flair for comedy!" said Brooke.

I couldn't help but laugh. A new Brooke? No such luck.